D0681878

KIDS' SPORTS STORIES

LOOK OUT, T-BALL!

by Shawn Pryor

illustrated by Amanda Erb

PICTURE WINDOW BOOKS
a capstone imprint

Kids' Sports Stories is published by Picture Window Books, an imprint of Capstone.
1710 Roe Crest Drive, North Mankato, Minnesota 56003
www.capstonepub.com

Copyright © 2020 by Capstone. All rights reserved. No part of this publication may be reproduced in whole or in part, or stored in a retrieval system, or transmitted in any form or by any means, electronic, mechanical, photocopying, recording, or otherwise, without written permission of the publisher.

Library of Congress Cataloging-in-Publication Data is available on the Library of Congress website.
ISBN 978-1-5158-4810-3 (library binding)
ISBN 978-1-5158-5880-5 (paperback)
ISBN 978-1-5158-4811-0 (eBook PDF)

Summary: Marlon knows he's not the best player on his T-ball team, but he can't understand why he's striking out at the sport, especially when he tries so hard. Teammate Anna offers to practice with him and soon sees why Marlon can't focus.

Designer: Ted Williams

Printed in the United States of America.
PA100

TABLE OF CONTENTS

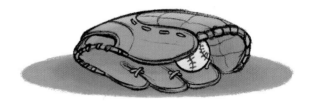

Glossary

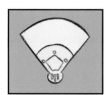 **infield**—the part of a playing field that holds the bases

 **outfield**—the grassy area beyond where the bases are (the infield)

 **strike**—a ball at which a batter swings and misses

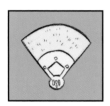 **tee**—a stand that holds a ball for a T-ball batter

 **umpire**—an official who makes sure a game is played correctly and fairly

Chapter 1

MARLON STRIKES OUT

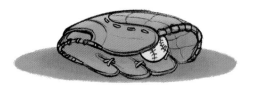

Marlon stood in the outfield. He and his teammates were playing their third game of the T-ball season.

"Be ready, Tigers! This batter can hit!" Coach said.

Marlon started to sweat. "Please don't hit the ball to me," he said quietly.

The other team's batter looked at the ball on the tee. He took a swing and—

BINK!

The ball soared into the outfield. Marlon raised his glove. He yelled, "I got it!"

But Marlon didn't get it. The ball flew just past his glove and dropped to the grass. His teammates groaned.

Marlon picked up the ball and tossed it toward second base. "Sorry," he said.

Later in the game, the Tigers were down to their last out. The bases were loaded. Marlon was at bat. He needed to hit the ball past the infield. If he did that, the Tigers would win.

"You can do it, Marlon!" his teammate Anna shouted.

But his teammate Kevin said, "No, he can't. He'll strike out again."

Marlon took a deep breath and stared at the ball. He took a big swing.

He missed.

"Strike one!" said the umpire.

Marlon tried again.

"Strike two!" the umpire yelled.

Marlon swung a third time. For the third time, he missed.

"Strike three, you're out! That's the game," said the umpire.

Marlon lowered his head. Some of his teammates grumbled.

"Told you he couldn't do it," Kevin said to Anna. "He's the worst player on our team."

Marlon heard what Kevin said. Those words made Marlon feel awful.

Chapter 2
HELP WANTED

After the game, Anna walked over to Marlon.

"Don't listen to Kevin," Anna said. "I know you can get better."

Marlon didn't believe her. "No I won't," he said. "I'm the worst player on the team, and nobody likes me."

Anna smiled. "I like you," she said.

"You do?" said Marlon.

"I do! And I'm going to help you," Anna said. "Come by my house tomorrow. We'll work on your catching and hitting."

"Great! Thank you, Anna! See you tomorrow!" Marlon said.

The next day, Marlon and Anna practiced together.

"Try getting a ground ball," said Anna. "Get in front of it and put your glove down."

Anna hit a ground ball. Marlon moved in front of it and put his glove down. But the ball rolled right by him.

"Whoops, sorry!" Marlon said.

"It's OK. Try another one," Anna said.

She hit a second ground ball. It rolled by
Marlon again.

That's when Anna noticed something.
Marlon squinted every time he went for
the ball.

"Marlon, try to catch this pop-up. Get under the ball and put your glove up," Anna said. She hit the ball high in the air.

Marlon looked for the ball. He squinted. A couple seconds later, it dropped to the ground behind him.

Marlon threw down his glove. "I can't do it! I keep messing up!" he said.

Anna held up her hand. "Marlon, how many fingers do you see?" she asked.

Marlon squinted again. "Four!" he shouted.

"No, it's one," Anna said. "Now
I see the problem! You can't see the
ball clearly!"

Chapter 3
EYE ON THE BALL

At the Tigers' next game, things were different. Marlon had a new look.

"Hey, you got glasses!" said Kevin.

Marlon smiled and nodded. "I went to the eye doctor," he said. "Close-up things looked clear to me, but everything else looked fuzzy. I can see a lot better now with my glasses."

"I helped him pick them out. I think they look awesome," Anna said.

"Thanks again, Anna," Marlon said.

"No problem," Anna said. "Let's win this game!"

Marlon's turn at bat came early. He picked up his bat and took a deep breath. He stared at the ball on the tee. It didn't look fuzzy at all! He took a swing and—

BINK!

Marlon got a hit! His teammates cheered as he ran to first base. It was a great start to the game.

Later, though, when the other team was at bat, Marlon missed a ball. It rolled right through his legs.

"Sorry! I didn't put my glove down!" Marlon shouted.

"It's OK! You'll get the next one!" Anna yelled back.

Near the end of the game, the Tigers took the lead. The other team had two outs and a runner on third base.

The batter for the other team stood by the tee. He swung. *BINK!* The ball flew into the outfield. Marlon's teammates called to him. "Get it, Marlon! Stay with it!" they yelled.

Marlon ran toward the ball. It looked sharp and clear, thanks to his new glasses.

He held up his glove.

The ball came down fast. Marlon watched it the whole way . . . right into his glove. *PLOP!* He squeezed his glove tight.

Marlon caught the ball! The Tigers
won the game!

Marlon's teammates ran to him and buried him in a big hug. "Look out, T-ball! Marlon's here to win!" Kevin shouted.

PLAY PICKLE!

In T-ball, sometimes a runner gets stuck between two bases. He or she is caught between two fielders, and one has the ball. You could say the runner is "in a pickle."

T-ball players often practice base running by playing the game of Pickle.

What You Need:
- an open grassy area, three players, two bases, two baseball gloves, and one ball

What You Do:
1. Place the bases about 25 steps apart.
2. Choose one player to be the runner. The runner should stand at the middle spot between the bases.
3. Each fielder should stand near a base. One should have the ball.
4. To start the game, the fielder without the ball shouts "Go!" The runner runs toward one base or another, and the fielders toss the ball back and forth or chase after the runner. The runner is out if he or she is tagged with the ball before reaching a base.
5. If the runner makes it safely to a base, he or she gets a point and takes another turn as runner. The runner always starts in the middle.
6. Change positions every time the runner is tagged out.

REPLAY IT

Take another look at this illustration. How do you think Marlon felt as he waited for the pop-up? What did he see and hear? What was he thinking?

Now pretend you're Marlon. Write a note to Anna that tells her about this big moment.

ABOUT THE AUTHOR

Shawn Pryor is the creator and co-author of the graphic novel mystery series Cash & Carrie, co-creator and author of the 2019 GLYPH-nominated football/drama series Force, and author of *Kentucky Kaiju* and *Jake Maddox: Diamond Double Play*. In his free time, he enjoys reading, cooking, listening to streaming music playlists, and talking about why Zack from the Mighty Morphin Power Rangers is the greatest superhero of all time.

ABOUT THE ILLUSTRATOR

Amanda Erb is an illustrator from Maryland currently living in the Boston, Massachusetts, area. She earned a BFA in illustration from Ringling College of Art and Design. In her free time, she enjoys playing soccer, learning Spanish, and discovering new stories to read.